planet of the bears

by giles andreae

original illustrations by janet cronin

EGMONT

EGMONT

We bring stories to life

First published in Great Britain 2011 by Egmont UK Limited
239 Kensington High Street, London W8 6SA

Text copyright © Portobello Rights Limited 2011
Illustrations © Portobello Rights Limited and the BBC 2011,
taken from the BBC series 'World of Happy by Giles Andreae'
based on original illustrations by Janet Cronin

Giles Andreae has asserted his moral rights

A CIP catalogue record for this title is available from the British Library

ISBN 978 1 4052 5845 6
1 3 5 7 9 10 8 6 4 2
Printed in Italy

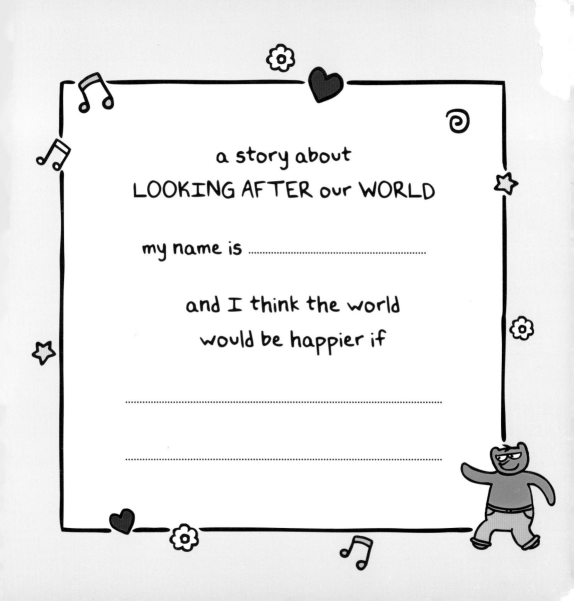

a story about
LOOKING AFTER our WORLD

my name is ....

and I think the world
would be happier if

....

....

The bears had all the STUFF they needed.

Yet still they wanted MORE.

But then one Clever Bear said, "Look!
Our planet's DYING! I think this
STUFF is killing it, my friends."

"But bears NEED STUFF,"
the bears all cried.

"Then why are you not HAPPY?"
the Clever Bear replied.

And just then something MAGICAL
occurred. A Mother Bear picked up
her baby and she beamed with JOY.

The Clever Bear ran over with a jar and closed it on the VAPOUR of her smile.

He PLANTED it . . .

and instantly bright flowers BLOOMED.

"That's it!" he said. "Instead of making STUFF, we bears must manufacture LOVE!

Assail your fellow bears with KINDNESS
and bottle just a bit each time for me."

Soon the Clever Bear had
filled a GIANT jar with love.

He travelled to the planet's HEART . . .
and planted it inside.

The Planet of the Bears is now AWASH with LIFE.

And all the bears are HAPPY.

And all the STUFF is gone.